Flash Digest

January 2025

Edited by
Terrie Leigh Relf

*

THE STAFF OF FLASH DIGEST

EDITOR: Terrie Leigh Relf
WEBMASTER: H. David Blalock
COVER DESIGNERS: Laura Givens; Marcia A. Borell

Cover art "Guardian" by Paula Hammond
Cover design by Laura Givens

Vol. II, No.1   January 2025

Contents

Features

Stories

Illustrations

THERE'S A SALE GOING
ON!!!
IT'S STILL GOING ON!!!

BUY ALL THE BOOKS YOU
WANT AND USE THIS 20%
DISCOUNT CODE:
BOOKS2024

THIS DISCOUNT CAN BE
USED AS MANY TIMES AS
YOU WISH, SO TAKE
ADVANTAGE OF IT!

GO TO OUR SHOP AT
WWW.HIRAETHSFFH.COM

NO MASKS, NO WAITING,
AND WE NEVER CLOSE!

A Little Help, Please

In the world of the small indie press we fight a never-ending battle for attention to our work, as writers and in publishing. Here's an example: big publishers [you know who they are] have gobs of $$$ that they can devote to advertising and marketing. Here at Hiraeth Publishing, our advertising budget consists of the deposits for whatever soda bottles and aluminum cans we can find alongside the highways. Anti-littering laws make our task even more difficult . . . ☺

That's where YOU come in. YOU are our best promoter. YOU are the one who can tell others about us. Just send 'em to our website, tell them about our store. That's all. Just that.

Of course, we don't mind if you talk us up. We're pretty good, you know. We have some award-winning and award-nominated writers and artists, plus other voices well-deserving to be heard [not everyone wins awards, right?] but our publications are read-worthy nevertheless.

That number once again is:

www.hiraethsffh.com

Friend us on Facebook at Hiraeth Publishing

Follow us on Twitter at @HiraethPublish1

The Sisterhood of
the Blood Moon
By Terrie Leigh Relf

For thousands of Earth years, the Transgalactic Consortium has had an invested interest in this planet and its inhabitants, the Haurans. While the Sisterhood of the Blood Moon and the Guardians work together with the Consortium and Haurans to restore balance to the universe, the Blood Moon is fast approaching. The power of this moon reveals untold secrets . . . including the sacred covenant with the Mora Spiders. There is an ancient pact that continues to be honored - but at what cost and for whose purpose?

The world may come to an end. But will there be a chance for a new beginning? And if so, where?

Type: Novel – science fiction/fantasy
Cover price: $14.95
ISBN: 9781087929927

Ordering link:
Print Edition:
https://www.hiraethsffh.com/product-page/sisterhood-of-the-blood-moon-by-terrie-leigh-relf

The Saint and the Demon

By t.santitoro & Ron Sparks

In the not-to-distant future, a young reporter reluctantly agrees to interview a senile old man in the heart of the Florida Everglades. In the humid, swampy environment, the reporter is sure that there can be no story of substance here, but the old man reveals that, in the past, his love was so strong and so passionate for a woman that he stopped at nothing to get her back when the forces of war tore them apart. He became a hero and a coward, a lover and a fighter . . . a saint and a devil. In his quest to rescue the woman he loved, he became something that she could no longer love.

Into the middle of this personal ordeal tumbles Cutter, a man from another world, sent to Earth to establish a breeding mission for his endangered race. He falls in love with an Earth woman, and must defend not only her, but also the future of his own people. The object of his alien affections, an innocent young woman named Angel, finds herself suddenly thrust into a world of aliens and intrigue, and of a love that has far more dangerous consequences than she could possibly have imagined.

Type: Novel – science fiction

Ordering Link:
Print ($13.95): https://www.hiraethsffh.com/product-page/saint-and-the-demon-by-t-santitoro-and-ron-sparks
PDF ($4.99): https://www.hiraethsffh.com/product-page/saint-the-demon-by-t-santitoro-ron-sparks
ePub ($4.99): https://www.hiraethsffh.com/product-page/saint-amp-the-demon-by-t-santitoro-amp-ron-sparks

The Gifted
By Tyree Campbell

DEDICATED TO THE MEMORY OF MELISSA MEAD

The year is 2045. Earth's societies have fallen apart for various reasons—economic, social, political, disease. To live, people began to loot, kill each other, and generally get by from day to day. In the latter stages of this deterioration, fear of disease caused immunizations to be rushed into production without proper testing. Some parents soon discovered that the children born were deformed in some way: flippers for hands and/or feet, missing organs, scales for skin, etc.

In addition to flippered hands and feet, Wendy Meade was gifted with some psi abilities that enabled her to talk with animals and with people. Now an adult woman, she scrapes by in a woods above a bay on the coast of southern Oregon, where there is an abandoned town where food is still available in convenience stores. She supplements this with shellfish from the bay. Such is her life.

Until one day she discovers that she can telepath with animals and people. A small community begins to form around her. Now, if possible, she has to use her powers to protect them from marauders.

Type: Post-Apocalyptic Novel
Ordering links:
Print: https://www.hiraethsffh.com/product-page/gifted-by-tyree-campbell
ePub: https://www.hiraethsffh.com/product-page/gifted-by-tyree-campbell-1
PDF: https://www.hiraethsffh.com/product-page/gifted-by-tyree-campbell-2

We Do What We Must
Denise Hatfield

Nobody ever really mentioned the smell when it came to the vast amounts of zombie apocalypse literature; at least in none that I had read before shit hit the fan. That's what I grumble as I sit on the top of Eaton Roads Hill overlooking the Westside of Hamilton. Nothing alive in the sense that I am, moves down in the city. The wind ruffles the overgrown foliage around me.

Aside from the zombies, at least the plants are well fed and flourish. The dead seem to only be driven by insatiable hunger and the virus in them, hell bent on spreading. The air around me is entrenched with rot and death that is as palpable as a heavy blanket. I'm convinced if I inhaled hard enough I would surely suffocate.

What I'd give for a breath of fresh air. Crunching brush and a moan later, tell me that I'm not alone. A zombie trips and face plants the asphalt behind me. A giggle almost escapes my throat as the shambler regains its upright position and slowly continues on its way. A few seconds later a runner careens into it and they both go tumbling down the hill. They seemed completely oblivious to their audience. Information I file away for later reflection.

Who knew the undead apocalypse would grant us with both types of zombies that fiction writers dreamt up. The slow creepers and the screeching marathon runners. It had taken only two weeks for it to spread throughout the United States and another three for global domination. The virulent virus strain that became known as "God's Hand's" irrevocably and indiscriminately steam rolled everyone, and everything in its path. Almost every news outlet's banner on the screen towards the end of transmission read:

IT'S IN GOD'S HANDS NOW

I think he had very little to do with it. I think he checked out long before this ever happened. Some thought the world would end in biblical fire, nuclear war or some sort of atmospheric breakdown. No. It was a single use syringe shot that has decimated a good chunk of life on this planet as we know it. Herd immunity turned into a mass extinction event. Whoever the shot didn't turn, its reciprocal creation, the zombies, did. I took up residence in the Lane library on North Third Street. It has been my haven for the last four years. I never thought I'd miss the sound of trains. The sound of silence used to be a comfort. Now I'd give anything to even hear a gun shot that I didn't fire. Multiple tables with many medical and survival books spread out everywhere is how I've made it this long. I spent many long hours reading a lot of jargon that I didn't understand and still don't. I've made it. Sometimes by uncomfortable and unsavory circumstances, but I'm still standing. For now.

The virus appears to spread through direct contact. Not through airborne pathways or vectors. The mosquitos alone would've got me that first summer the virus was loose, if the air didn't. This virus also seems to have made the jump to some animals. What animals I have seen, they're either down for the count or have been turned. I haven't had the chance to investigate that much other than observations. The few experiments I've managed to accomplish haven't yielded much. The turn time seems to vary. The eight subjects that were involuntarily part of the experiments were: Amber M., John H., John Doe, Jane Doe, Richard W., Craig, Alicia, and Philip. I have to refer to them as subjects, thinking of them as people makes what I've had do and still need to do, extremely difficult. Sometimes we do what we must. Even the most unfavorable and despicable things. I will not forget their names, the ones I knew of anyways. I won't forget the screams. I digress. It's best not to dwell on that.

Cutting off infected areas didn't work nor did trying to cut the area out. Amber turned immediately after being bit. It appeared like a nasty flu in John. He went eleven days before turning. John died twice in one day. Not every day do you get to say that. Everyone else turned either immediately or didn't last more than eleven days. So far. Richard is still in the basement. I'll see how long the dead can rot before motion is inhibited or they die again. Well, that's me being optimistic. Realistically, I won't, but stranger things have happened.

The other thing that some fiction didn't mention is how brutal and destructive the bites are. The wound on my left forearm burns and festers no matter how much I cut, clean or cauterize it. What remains of the tendons and muscles strain whenever I move it. I'm surprised that I still have movement capabilities in that appendage. It's day nine for me and the fever started two days ago. I don't know whether the fever induced hallucinations, infection or another zombie will do me in. Perhaps in a moment of clarity such as this one, the 9mm Sig on my hip will be my last supper. Eating a bullet doesn't sound so bad compared to my other options looming on the horizon. I flex my left arm which barely allows me to form a fist. I pull a dandelion from the ground next to me and wish for the umpteenth time for a breath of fresh air as I blow on it. Sending every hope, wish and dream I ever had floating on the foul summer breeze.

Living Bad Dreams
By Denise Hatfield

When dreams come alive, there's no telling where they will lead. Everything changes when you realize that, dream or no dream, you're going to die. What do you do then?

Ordering Link:
Print: https://www.hiraethsffh.com/product-page/living-bad-dreams-by-denise-hatfield-1
ePub: https://www.hiraethsffh.com/product-page/living-bad-dreams-by-denise-hatfield-2
PDF: https://www.hiraethsffh.com/product-page/living-bad-dreams-by-denise-hatfield

Mystic Librarian
By Sandy DeLuca

Mission Hephaestus V
Richard Schell

TOP SECRET

To: Admiral Millhoff
               Pentagon Space Security
From: Major T. D. Anderson
               NASA Liaison to the Pentagon

Summary: The *Hephaestus V* and the *Hephaestus Sentinel* systems serve the dual role of studying and giving early warning of near-earth asteroids and investigating interstellar bodies if and when they might appear. The mission began years after the 2017 appearance of the first observed interstellar object 1I 2017 U1, also known as Oumuamua.

Approximately seven weeks ago, the *Hephaestus V* mission was sent to coordinate with the crewless *Hephaestus Sentinel* system when the anomalous interstellar body 2I 070016 was discovered. The interstellar origin of the body was confirmed by observations of its speed and hyperbolic trajectory, which crossed through the plane of our solar ecliptic.

As you are aware, the *Hephaestus V Sentinels* are a series of crew-less probes sent up eight years ago to intercept on command any interesting near-earth objects if and when they were to appear and to collect data for analysis. As planned, the manned *Hephaestus V* mission left from Luna base #19 due to the unprecedented circumstances of our findings. From a position between the orbits of Earth and Mars, the manned mission was to coordinate with the sentinel and rendezvous to minimize the time delay required to communicate the mission findings. At the same time, the proximal sentinel had modified its course weeks before to position itself to intercept the object.

On arrival, the sentinel began measurements, showing the body to be approximately 300 meters long and 70 meters wide. However, because of the irregular reflective properties of the object, it was impossible to determine its shape in any great detail. The sentinel detected the venting of material from the surface, initially believed to be a coma of microscopic debris or ice crystals as is commonly seen in comets. However, observations showed that the debris became directed toward the sentinel probe shortly before it went offline. Coordinated efforts from NASA and the eight-member crew of *Hephaestus V* over the next six days failed to regain communication or control of the sentinel, and contact has yet to be restored.

During that week, the interstellar object rapidly moved out of range for any possible further observations. It continued its hyperbolic trajectory out of the solar system with minimal alteration from its expected course. In the meantime, in light of discussions with NASA, the eight-member crew of *Hephaestus V* received orders to return to Luna base #19.

For the next five days, the return trip back to the moon was uneventful under the command of Captain Quansah. On day six, optical and radio anomalies were observed originating from the direction of the object. The crew noted a tiny diffuse cloud of debris, which followed and then overtook the ship.

The following day, all systems of the *Hephaestus V* were evaluated and found to be fully functional as they continued on their course to Luna base #19. A day later, Lieutenant Lyou noted a surface anomaly while performing an optical diffraction exam of the vessel's hull. The crew performed structural analyses, and they all tested within specifications. As an additional precaution, the Captain ordered the *Hephaestus* engineering repair drone, HERD, to survey the exterior. There were no new findings that were found.

The following day, the engineer, Dr. Gillespie, shared her concerns about the HERD drone. She detected a subtle but unmistakable change in the metallic sheen of the drone, confirmed by the identical optical diffraction measurements used on the hull. While the drone passed all diagnostic tests, concerns remained.

Gillespie shared another suspicious finding with the Captain. The generative AI computer in the ship is so sophisticated that an almost human-like complexity emerged from the system. Any unusual changes in behavior would be recognized by an experienced user, just as one would detect an imposter of a close friend. Gillespie noted that shortly after encountering the debris cloud of the object, she noticed subtle anomalies in the ship's computer. This finding troubled Gillespie.

After further investigation, she removed the central processor from the HERD. When she applied enough heat to destroy it, she witnessed a shimmering red blur over its entire surface. After replacing it on the drone, it performed exactly as if nothing had been done. She reported her observations but did not provide an explanation based on any known earthly technology. It was as if the entire ship had been replaced with unknown alien technology without the crew's awareness. Could the object have sent a cloud capable of taking over and re-engineering the vessel, like a virus taking over a host cell?

Later that evening, after many hours of double-checking and discussing, Gillespie and the Captain contacted NASA Control Center using a highly secure encrypted line isolated from the rest of the ship. Gillespie ingeniously used a coding system she and Timothy Chin from the NASA control center had developed during their graduate school years. She was confident that Timothy would easily recognize the code and be able to decode the message in secret.

In that communication, she shared her observations and dire concerns about the mission. She stated that the self-diagnostic tests of the ship's main computer and the AI system failed to uncover any errors. However, other observations that Gillespie detected could not be explained other than by some unexplainable manipulation of hardware and software. They concluded that an alien modification of the entire vessel was the only explanation they were left to consider. This possible interpretation suggests that anything, by merely contacting a portion of the *Hephaestus V* could, in turn, be cannibalized by technology under alien control.

That was the final message we received from the crew of *Hephaestus V*. We have been unable to contact the ship for over 48 hours since our last contact. Over that time, we noted that the craft had changed course and was now no longer headed toward Luna base #19. It has changed course for Earth.

Please advise us on your next steps in light of these extraordinary and unprecedented events. After extensive analysis by our team here at Flight

Control, we have no explanation other than the one proposed by the lost crew of *Hephaestus V*.

Red Forest Woman
By Sandy DeLuca

Once More, With Feeling

Tyree Campbell

The thunderstorm rolled in from the northwest, a ravenous amorph from another universe bent on engulfing all in its path and taking it back home. I could hear it growling, my thoughts as dark and roiled as the rain-gravid clouds themselves. In the maudlin vulnerability of the winter ale and summer sausage I'd downed earlier in the evening, I laughed and cried, unable to sleep. So many shouldas, wouldas, couldas. Remorse induces insomnia, and I was an underachiever, the revelation in my cups. Oh, what I might have done with my life. And the whatever-happened-to's chimed in with their own laments. In an alcoholic haze I'd Googled for my high school girlfriend--but there were just too many Larsons in San Diego. No retakes or do-overs for me.

What dreams were left to me, now, at this late date? Might I sleep, perchance to dream? Or was I better off making a quick end of it, and let the last perchance fade to black with me?

The wind picked up. Through the drapes came flashes of light, followed by distant snaps, crackles, pops, and bangs, that put the computer downstairs at risk. I knew I ought to unplug it, but I deferred to the next flashes, and the next--if the storm drew any closer, I'd go down . . . if the thunder grew too loud, I'd go down. While I silently chanted this mantra the wind pierced the clematis in the trellis outside the window like a flock of shrikes, and the leaves ticked against the aluminum siding. The growling of the storm grew louder. In the dark I looked up at the ceiling. How far could lightning penetrate into a house?   At another flash through the window I flinched, and covered my head with a pillow. If I couldn't see the flashes, I would be safe.   That wasn't the ale talking. I'd always believed that, and for no good reason save that it was the easiest defense. Cover up and don't move, and the Goths of Life won't get you.

Rain sang off the roof, and bits of ice spilled like gravel onto the yard and the street and the Pontiac.   All the symptoms of a tornado were present, but I heard no warning sirens. Was the city blind? Could they not see the sky?

Or was this storm meant for me alone?

I drew the cocoon of blankets up over my head, and hoped the beets and carrots and tomatos and beans in the small garden behind the house would survive, hoped the lilac and wisteria blossoms would remain intact after such a beating. The pillow and blankets failed to block the light, and nothing could muffle the rumbles. Flash-to-bang diminished to a count of ten, then five. The wind did not abate. I'd have to replant the garden, no doubt of that now...if I lived through the night. I drew my legs up and huddled there among the ghosts of a wasted past.

The storm seemed to pause for a moment, as if debating whether to include me in its diet. Then came a whoosh of wind that rattled the eaves, and a static discharge of light so thick I saw it through the pillow. Two seconds later, God's fist hammered the ground.

An unearthly silence followed, as if the power transformer on the corner pole had been zapped and fused. The wind died out, and the rain and the hail, as if the house and its contents had been swept abruptly into a more tranquil universe. Spent, I fell asleep.

I dreamed of a fertile garden and of a shy woman tittering behind her hand, dark eyes glowing at me. I dreamed of sowing fresh seeds and planting fresh tomatoes. Somewhere, perhaps in the study or the music room, I was doing...something. I awoke, wondering what I had been doing.

I awoke, wanting to do it.

Light through the open drapes freshened the room. The morning's necessities completed, I went outside to inspect the garden for damage. The hail had flattened everything I had done...but I had more seeds and more plants. The garden would recover, in time. The sanguine realization rather astonished me. Where once I might have cursed and lamented, now I saw what might be done, if I but made the effort. Even the sun was supportive. It was ruddy vermillion this morning, although no haze shrouded it as it fought its way back from the darkness, taking time out from its journey to warm my back and soothe my spirit. Perhaps I, like it, would follow a course.

Nearby, beyond the low banks of lilacs to the west, a bird tittered, and I turned toward the sound. Beyond the shrubbery, two large moons poised to drop below the horizon. Two . . . so it had not been a storm that had taken me.

A second moon . . . a second chance . . .

From the other side of the lilacs again came tittering, and I saw dark eyes peering at me through the leaves.

Not a bird.

Heir Apparent
Tyree Campbell

Answering a distress call, March and Myrrha find a young woman who has deliberately been marooned on an uninhabited world. She claims to be Hoya Palologa, heir to the Palologa throne on Wanderby. But there is already a Hoya who has been invested as the heir apparent to that throne. Myrrha believes the claim of the Hoya she and March have encountered. Thus begins a journey to establish the succession, a journey made far more perilous because Hoya not only claims the throne, but is also a sinister personage with several crimes on her resume.

March and Myrrha find themselves embroiled in internal politics on Wanderby, where the slightest wrong move can get them killed. The rulers on that world are oblivious to the subtle machinations of their underlings, one of whom has created a lookalike but false Hoya. Which one is which? And will death take the real one before March and Myrrha can stop it?

Type: Novel – science fiction

Ordering Links:
Print: https://www.hiraethsffh.com/product-page/heir-apparent-by-tyree-campbell
PDF: https://www.hiraethsffh.com/product-page/heir-apparent-by-tyree-campbell-2
ePub: https://www.hiraethsffh.com/product-page/heir-apparent-by-tyree-campbell-1

The Red Foil
By t.santitoro

When Soefee Sparrow's roommate and ex-lover, Tayla Block, goes missing aboard a space mining station, Sparrow—a rocket-horse jockey—suddenly finds herself under suspicion of murder.

Despite the mining company's main source of income—megatons of industrial minerals and gem stones—no one but Soefee seems to be searching for their leading geologist.

Were gemstones being stolen from the mining company? Did it have anything to do with Block's disappearance? Why was everyone being so tight-lipped?

What happened to Tayla Block, and why wasn't anything being done to find her?

Enter Jicob Elfrendini, an undercover agent for IBCP, a division of Law Enforcement employed to ensure against the theft of valuable gems. But Elfrendini has secrets of his own.

And then a woman's dead body is found at the bottom of a mine shaft and, together, Soefee and Jicob must work to find out who killed Tayla Block—

--and WHY?

Print: https://www.hiraethsffh.com/product-page/red-foil-by-t-santitoro
ePub: https://www.hiraethsffh.com/product-page/red-foil-by-t-santitoro-2
PDF: https://www.hiraethsffh.com/product-page/red-foil-by-t-santitoro-1

FCB

Barry O'Farrell

Police banged on the front door. Travis stalled. He was deliberately slow to respond. He yelled through the door, "I'm getting the key." They continued to yell "Open Up, police. Open Up".

Dave knew what to do. He quietly asked, "Anyone got any warrants?" The group of online poker players looked up from their machines and shook their heads unanimously.

"Abe, you sure?"

"Sure, I'm sure.

"Anyone got any computer chips? Gimmicked chips? Counterfeit chips?" Again, a round of negative head shaking.

"Georgie, guns?"

"Stashed. Safe deposit box. Bank," whispered the ever quiet George.

"Jay, are you stashing anything?"

"Nope," from Jay.

"Maria, identity stuff from the Dark Web?"

"Not this time."

"Or fake passports. Maria, someone else's credit cards? Fake passports?"

"Not today."

Dave remembered something. "Jay, are you stashing for someone else?"

"Hell no."

Travis reluctantly unlocked and opened the door. Police entered: two in uniform, two plain clothes. Senior detective led the way. The second detective, young and scrawny, clutched a tablet to his chest. Looked too young to be a detective.

***

"No-one ain't got no warrants," Dave stated.

The detective asked, "Who is Abraham Powell?"

"Me," acknowledged Abe confident of his innocence.

"Arrest him," directed the detective. The uniform cops seized an arm each.

"For what? I haven't done nothin'," pleaded Abe, "Your name and shield number, copper."

"Detective Strong. Shield 712, this is Detective Bartlett 5229." Bartlett raised his tablet in acknowledgement. "We are from the FCB, Future Crime Bureau. We are arresting you for your next crime."

"Say what?"

"It's what we do. Prevent. Detective Bartlett will explain."

"My model," began the nerdy Bartlett addressing the room, "predicts 12 months in advance. It shows your next crime. Or crimes."

"Oh yeah. What's my future crime anything?" dared Abe, head up, chin out.

Bartlett ignored Abe's question. "Applies to everyone in this room. We have a RNM program, Relationship Network Monitoring. The program monitors your network. It knows who knows who, introductions, changes and so forth.

"Combine this with each individual's criminal skills," continued Bartlett," plus preferences derived from previous behaviour, plus likely behaviour . . . plus thoughts, yes thoughts, leads us to all the people in this room."

Stunned silence from the group.

"Cuff him," directed Strong with a snap of his fingers.

"Look at the old style handcuffs. Hi-tech crap but low-tech handcuffs. Where's your electro cuffs. No budget?" drawled Travis sarcastically.

"Sounds like crap to me," uttered Dave waving a hand in a wave it off motion.

"Sounds like crap to me, too," echoed Maria, "and I know computers. Where do you get this stuff from?"

"SoC," snapped Bartlett.

"Say again?" asked Maria cocking her head to the left.

"SoC, System on a Chip," Bartlett replied, "lots of them."

"Never heard of it."

"Not as computer smart as you thought you were, Miss Computer Einstein," jibed Strong, enjoying her comeuppance. "Maria Delvecchio, much travelled, self-styled fashionista. Unfortunate tattoos in unfortunate places. Regret them now, don't cha? We know the ones." Maria looked away and pulled her jacket closed.

"Program includes Failure Prediction. AI identifies probability for fail," resumed Bartlett warming to his specialty. "I mean it looks for human behaviour failure. Your behaviour," turning to face Dave," David Brooks, you started changing early. You became a crook, young."

"Prevention," from detective Strong, "Prevention is better than investigate after the crime has been committed."

Bartlett chimed in with, "Investigation after the fact. Expensive. Time consuming. Messy."

"Prevention is now. Get him into the Transport Bubble. Get him out of here."

"You'll be hearing from my lawyer," yelled Abe angrily, "you haven't heard the last of this future bullshit."

"Everyone else sit still," commanded Bartlett. "I'll take your facial recognition and image recognition both."

"For what?" from Maria.

"For Infra Data and Cloud."

"Gets you what?"

"Ah . . . yes . . . the combination produces all sorts of things. Your preferred Sunday lunch. Your next tattoo. Sound recognition, too: Omniverse audio2Face AI, matches voices with images you filmed for social media."

"You're kidding," blurted Travis in disbelief.

"Anomaly Detection," continued Bartlett. "Anomaly Detection is constantly comparing anomalies to a person's usual behaviour, changes to personal schedules and common contacts. Useful in pre-detecting planned crimes. Central computer will run the data we have on you against my model. Never know what you might be up to in the next 12 months. Sit still."

Strong stroked his chin but remained silent. He wished the geek-speak would stop.

"SoC," muttered Maria to herself.

The usually quiet Georgie glanced at her and whispered, "Homework. Where are you going to research SoC?"

***

Detective Strong was quiet for the early part of the drive to Bureau headquarters. There was a lot to take in with this new technology. He wondered where it would lead in time. How to manage it? Where did old fashion detective work fit in? Where did he fit in?

Detective Bartlett worked on his tablet in silence.

Finally, Strong spoke. "This program of yours, predictions work all the time?"

"Yes . . . well, but with a couple of exceptions. Crimes of passion. Spontaneous. No lead up anything. Someone snaps. Stuff like that."

"Weapons of Mass Destruction. Who's got the bomb?" asked Strong changing subject.

"Good question. Well . . . with your experience or intuition, I thought you might have identified the most likely suspect today."

"Didn't. No fanatic. What does your program say now we have seen them?"

"No bomb. Let me check a couple of things." The screen of Bartlett's tablet rolled over. "Jay T. Gardner the Third. Most probably has componentry. Or can supply componentry. No bomb thrower there."

"Have we frightened off the bomber?" posed Strong hopefully, thinking out loud.

"Doubt it."

"What about the quiet one, Georgie? The quiet ones worry me."

"Yeh. Don't worry. Looks like George will be taken out," predicted Bartlett.

"Really? Anyone we know?"

Bartlett double checked his tablet. "Uhm . . . well . . . hmm, interesting. Program reads: Probability car crash. Probability fleeing a shootout."

"Plausible."

"Uhm, it's a pity about Maria's next overseas trip, too. Third world prison conditions and all."

Movie review: Lola

By **LEE CLARK ZUMPE**

In October 2015, the New York Times Magazine sparked a Twitter frenzy when it posted the results of a poll in which it asked readers "Could You Kill a Baby Hitler?" By no means an original concept, it presented the hypothetical query in seemingly simplistic terms designed to trigger knee-jerk responses that separated respondents into specific camps.

Time-travel vigilantes were in the majority, with 42% ready to transport themselves to the town of Braunau am Inn in Austria-Hungary in 1889 to commit infanticide. Not quite one-third — 30% — said no, and another 28% said "not sure."

Of course, it's tempting. Hitler, dictator of Germany and leader of the Nazi Party, was directly responsible for the Holocaust — which resulted in the deaths of 6 million Jews in concentration and extermination camps, as well as the deaths of 220,000-500,000 Romani people, 200,000-250,000 disabled individuals, 1.8 million Polish civilians, 7 million Soviet citizens, and an estimated 3,100 to 3,600 members of the LGBTQ community. Those figures don't include the number of military personnel who died in the largest and most violent military conflict in human history.

Does the knowledge of what will happen provide justification for our time-traveling vigilantes to kill an innocent baby? And must the question be framed in such a way that excludes equally efficient strategies by putting the newborn on a different path?

For academicians, engaging in thoughtful counterfactual history can provide insight into how historical events transpired, and reveal connections that may have gone otherwise unnoticed. It is a form of reactionary thought experiment that begins with a simple "what if" question. For science fiction writers, it provides the basis for alternate history storylines.

"Lola," an Irish-British found footage science fiction film directed by Andrew Legge, is the most recent manifestation of counterfactual history in cinema. "Lola" opened in select theaters and on demand on Aug. 4.

The film is set predominantly in 1941. Nazi Germany's conquest of Europe is already underway, and France and the Low Countries have fallen. Nightly air raids are conducted on British cities, Royal Air Force airbases, and radar stations as Hitler tries to gain air superiority prior to launching an invasion of Britain.

Two sisters, living in an English country house, have designed a machine that can intercept radio and TV broadcasts from the future. Thomasina "Thom" Hanbury (Emma Appleton) is the eccentric, troubled genius who created the machine. Her sister, Martha "Mars" Hanbury (Stefanie Martini), initially focuses on using it to glimpse landmarks of the anti-establishment cultural phenomenon and future achievements that seem to suggest a "great, big, beautiful tomorrow" right out of Walt Disney's Carousel of Progress.

Thom and Mars use the machine — which they name "Lola" after their mother — to monitor broadcasts to determine the time and location of upcoming raids, warning residents ahead of time to minimize casualties. Mars issues warnings anonymously, and the press and public soon dub her "the Angel of Portobello."

Eventually, the military locates the sisters and convinces them that the machine could be put to better use to deploy air defenses. Assigning Lieutenant Sebastien Holloway (Rory Fleck Byrne) to work with the sisters, a plan is enacted. In little time, the intel gleaned from future broadcasts on the machine enables the British military to effectively put an end to the Blitz. Having scored one victory, the military pushes for intel that will give them an edge against the Kriegsmarine — and, more specifically, wolfpacks of German U-boats that threatened to cut off war supplies and food bound for England.

This is where the mad scientist trope materializes. Thom becomes so obsessed with proving Lola's capacity to change history that she puts an American vessel at risk. Unforeseen repercussions from the event create catastrophic changes to the timeline.

As the viewer watches the early successes of the sisters, it becomes increasingly evident that the other shoe will soon drop. In "Lola," that shoe is a jackboot. Thom and Mars are separated, the Nazis invade England, and the future is a fascist nightmare — unless Mars, who has come to understand the terrible consequences of Lola's power — can find a way to fix everything.

It's difficult not to notice similarities between "Lola" and one of the most celebrated episodes of "Star Trek: The Original Series." In "The City on the Edge of Forever," written by Harlan "Pay the Writer" Ellison, Leonard McCoy (DeForrest Kelley), Captain Kirk (William Shatner) and Spock (Leonard Nimoy) end up in 1930s New York City during the Great Depression after encountering the Guardian of Forever, a sentient time portal. McCoy, who was the first to travel back in time, has done something that altered history. Kirk and Spock must determine what McCoy changed and set things back on course. They soon discover that Edith Keeler (Joan Collins), a soup kitchen operator, will establish a pacifist movement that keeps the United States from intervening in World War II, allowing Nazi Germany to overrun Europe and develop the first atomic bomb.

Despite script revisions that led to a long-running feud between Ellison and Star Trek creator Gene Roddenberry, "The City on the Edge of Forever" is considered one of the best episodes of the original series and one of the best stories of the franchise. It is tragic, terrifying, and insightful. Like "Lola," it asks, "What if," and follows a trail of seismic shifts stemming from one seemingly inconsequential incident.

"Lola" also follows the ripples that radiate from each change in history. Cleverly constructed, Legge went to great lengths to make his found footage film feel authentic. Some Scenes were reportedly shot on 16mm Bolex and Arriflex cameras with period lenses. Newsreel sequences were shot on a 1930s Newman Sinclair 35mm wind-up camera on Kodak Double X film.

There are intentional anachronisms scattered throughout the film, as the sisters adopt slang terms from future era, such as "cool" and "groovy." There are also accidental anachronisms, such as a reference to B movies mentioned in describing the footage displayed by Lola.

The viewer will have difficulty finding empathy for Thom and Mars. Appleton and Martini never quite fit into the milieu as persuasively as is needed to make this alternate history piece work. It comes off as shoddy cosplay at times. The detached performance of the two main characters and contrivances of story diminish the impact of an ambitious script.

"Lola" is well-intentioned, meticulously researched, and cunningly crafted. It is full of big ideas and fascinating extrapolations. It posits a powerful case for critical thinking for those willing to pay close attention. Legge's morality play shows how hasty decisions may beget dangerous consequences. It reminds us how fascism masquerades as patriotism, and how it cloaks itself in libertarian phrases and righteousness while infecting the masses with authoritarian, ultranationalist ideology. It expects individuals to succumb to knee-jerk reactions and give in to negative emotions that generate narrow-mindedness and intolerance.

If you are willing to overlook the many shortcomings that may be attributed to a low budget, "Lola" succeeds in conveying an important message in a highly imaginative and evocative way.

The Chicken Dilemmas
Scott Virtes

Farmer AXJ47 stood over his damaged robot chicken across the highway from his farm complex. He gleamed in the sun, trying to compute this odd happening, while hovercars whizzed past . . . so many minds, going who-knows-where, and gone in a flash.

The farmer bot wasn't interested in how the chicken got out of the factory. That was easy. There had been a small flaw in the fence. The question was how it ended up HERE. Luckily, cars don't touch the road anymore—hard to believe anyone (or anything) ever traveled that way. Still, the cars' suspension fields were a serious threat. The fields would have cooked a real chicken, and managed to scramble this chicken-unit's brain.

The question was: *Why did the chicken cross the road?*

Suddenly, AXJ47 was bombarded with images, a bit-torrent of illogical fragments. He saw long-extinct humans on stages asking that same question, felt megadata pour through his body from old archives. His firewalls sprang into action, and he was rooted to the spot for several minutes while he ran internal scans and validated his wireless connections.

What was that all about?

His systems told him there had been no virus, no actual threat. He queried the data net more carefully. How many different answers were there to this simple question?

"542,394. WARNING: This data set has a high entropy rating. It is mostly from obsolete sources, many of which may have been damaged. Proceed with caution."

Okay. The data net of the machine world was built upon the earlier data net of the human world, and these wildly conflicting answers came from beyond the "membrane," that fine split between the old and new data sets. Apparently, humans had a hard time answering this question.

Analyze . . .

AXJ47 found himself frozen again while his defenses mopped up another logic spill inside his brain. Whatever this human data set was trying to say, the only thing consistent about it was its high nonsense ranking. The data wasn't damaged, it was just . . . garbage? It wasn't a virus, it was just . . . idiotic?

He asked the local data lord to reduce the whole mess to a useful packet. "Why did the chicken cross the road?"

A moment later he received an answer: "I don't know. Why don't you ask the chicken?"

It was so simple. The robot farmer wondered why the old humans didn't simply ask their chickens. He picked up his chicken unit. A quick scan showed that it wasn't seriously damaged. After a quick reboot, he asked the chicken the question. After all, if something about the highway attracted any escaping livestock, he'd have to build more fences.

The chicken promptly exploded.

AXJ47 stood there holding the charred stump of a cyberfowl.

"That's enough!" He said. He had wasted too much time with this silly problem. He had eggs to ship. He told his data interface to isolate him from that problematic query and all associated queries.

There was only one other query with the same hazard profile: *Which came first, the chicken or the egg?*

The robot farmer jetted off the ground calmly, and headed up over the highway.

"Well, obviously it was the egg. Old earth chickens came from eggs, right?"

Halfway across the hissing line of cars, he thought again. "No, eggs came from chickens. Simple oviparous reproduction. Supplemental information: Chicken eggs came from something that was mostly chicken, from a genetic viewpoint. But if that thing wasn't a chicken (Note: Species is not a precisely defined term), it was a . . . "

His lifeless body tumbled to the ground in between two speeding hover-lorries. His manager-bot found him there the next day, docked him some pay, and gave him a jump-start. AXJ47 had a semantic breakdown and refused to work near chickens or eggs ever again. His whole agricultural RAM had to be wiped, and he was transferred to an ice-cracking plant outside of what was once Green Bay.

Deep in the data net, other bits of old human comedy— miscatalogued as science—were waiting to score one for the team. The last human scientist had said something important, right before being atomized on the White House lawn. Although the robot data-masses suppressed it, thinking it daring to erase that man's last words, what he said was: "If you can't learn from the past, at least you've been programmed to choke on it."

The Contest Winner
Matthew Wilson

"Is the coast clear?"

Simon Kingdon didn't want to break into the circus but his friend, Peter Thomson, had threatened to expose him as a wimp in school the next day. Today was Sunday, the day famous for craziness and it had to be true because Peter said.

Simon could smell popcorn. The sign ahead said PRIVATE SHOWING

"You said you could break into fort Knox by now," he hated how small his voice sounded. Mom was right—Peter was a bad influence.

Snick.

"Relax." Peter opened his father's flick knife, hoping he looked cool and cut into the big top red fabric. The goons at the door said this show wasn't for children, but Peter was determined and had had the three week detention in Borstal to prove it.

"Open Sesame," he giggled. With scars on his fingers, he more carefully sheathed his blade than the last time.

Last and loyally, Simon dropped to his hands and knees, crawling through the hole. He almost screamed when balloons and bunting ruffled his hair.

Someone was having a party?

Simon could hear the cheering louder now that it wasn't muffled by the poster-coated fabric of the big top.

BE AMAZED BY THE STRONG MAN. BE FRIGHTENED BY THE HIDEOUS WOMAN.

The temptation was too much for Peter. He would not be denied something to post on his social media.

Simon tried to stand up until his knee creaked and he lay there behind the chairs until the ache subsided. The applauding audience were too engrossed in the show on stage to take any notice of them.

"The doors are locked and we can have our contest at last," said the man in the spotlight, the ringmaster holding a poster showing a cliche strongman wearing a caveman loincloth supporting two dumbbells over his bald head.

Simon covered his ears as the cheering increased. The strongman bounding onto the stage seemed to savour the attention.

"Is there anyone who can lift more than our friend here? This is supposed to be a contest after all."

Peter shushed Simon when three lovely ladies pushed a wagon on the stage, on top of which was a safe.

"That thing is just made of balloons." Peter rolled his eyes. "They've painted it grey to look the real deal, but that safe is as fake as that money I printed in art class."

"Three tonnes, ladies and gentlemen," the ringmaster cried out. "Is there anyone here who can beat the man from Galag forty-three. They don't have gravity there, you know."

Simon blinked. "Where?"

"You think I passed geography class? Hush up. I bet I can snag that trophy."

"Pete, no."

The crowd cheered again as three women appeared on stage, removed their robes, and Simon tasted sick as he saw their green scales. Their tongues flicked excitedly as they lay down on a bed of nails without harm.

"Let's see which Venus girl can last the longest," the ringmaster threw his black tall hat into the hair and caught it. "Their scales are like armour but even that won't save them forever. This is a contest, you know."

"Pete, this is crazy, we have to get out of here."

Simon could see where his friend was heading. Of course he wasn't going to compete on stage against the strong man—not with his weedy arms—but in the wings stood a table, left unoccupied by the stagehand who had wandered off for a cigarette.

On them rested several trophies scarred with inscriptions.

Hottest fire breath.
Quickest jump between dimensions
Longest days holding breath

"I'm not leaving empty handed," Peter said, but his feet lost momentum when he saw the old men floating in the big tops' ceiling weren't on trapeze wires.

"Who can fly the longest?" the ringmaster twisted his moustache, enjoying the drama.

Simon was scared now. Were the flying pensioners wizards? Was he going insane?

He felt the fabric walls closing in and his legs threatened to give out. He needed to get out.

Now!

Then when the crowd applauded with their tentacles, he screamed.

Someone grabbed him, his badge said "security," but he had four yellow eyes and two heads.

"A human?" his left head said. "There's a human in here."

"No, there's two humans in here," another guard said. Attracted by the commotion, he caught the leg of something scampering beneath the seats and shook Peter until the boy dropped all the trophies he clung to.

I'm dreaming, Simon thought, but his chest tightened as the ringmaster assured the murmuring crowd that things were fine. There was no need for refunds.

"This is a private event, humans. What are you doing here?" he demanded.

"I didn't want to come," Simon sobbed. "What's going on here?"

"Just a little friendly contest between monsters, aliens, and friends," the ringmaster said. "It's frustrating holding your truth back, knowing you can break any human but if they discover what you are, they'll send you back across the stars—if you're lucky. There's many an alien or werewolf in the crowd your kind would cut up in a lab. We only want a little fun, a competition to really let ourselves out—and now you've spoiled it."

I won't say anything, Simon wanted to say, but his mouth was dry as wool and he could only shake his head.

"You freaks won't get away with this," Peter said and Simon wished he hadn't.

"Cook them," shouted a vampire. "Cook them now."

"No," said the ringmaster. "This is supposed to be a competition. We see what Martians can do the best breakdancing, what Saturnese can make themselves invisible the quickest. But back on my home planet, we have a favourite contest of mine— who can eat the most children in sixty seconds."

The ringmaster smiled and opened his

mouth much wider than Simon had ever seen anyone do before.

Simon almost had time to scream before the minute started.